Dewdrop Babies

Sweetpea's Surprise

Patricia MacCarthy

PICTURE CORGI

Rose and Violet are in the Diamond Room. The shelves are filled with vases containing glistening dewdrops.

"Oh, look! They sparkle just like our bracelets!" says Rose.

They fill their watering cans with dewdrops and get ready to go to work.

"It's such a hot day today, our flowers will be very thirsty," says Violet.

The garden is buzzing with life. Insects dart to
and fro, and the birds are singing in the trees.

Violet skips off to look after her flower,
which grows at the bottom of the garden.
"See you later, Rose," she calls.

Rose's flower is beautiful and the soft,
pink petals give off a lovely smell.

Rose waters it, and polishes the leaves.
She has to be careful – there are lots of prickles!

Suddenly a green hairy wriggly thing pokes its head out of a rolled-up rose leaf.
Rose shrieks in fright.

"What are YOU?"

"I'm a caterpillar," says the hairy thing, "and I'm hungry. This leaf will make a tasty snack!"

"You can't eat my leaf!" squeals Rose.

"Just one," pleads the caterpillar, "and then I can stop eating!"

"Don't move. And don't eat! I'll be back!" says Rose as she dashes off to find Violet.

Rose finds Violet and tells her about the caterpillar. "What shall I do?"

"Let's go and ask Sweetpea," suggests Violet.
"She can look in *The Keepers of the Garden Guide Book*!"

Violet and Rose race back to the palace.

They find her in the library
and ask her what to do.

Sweetpea takes the *Guide
Book* from the shelf.

She turns to the section on caterpillars.

"Oh, yes, I see," she mutters.

"What do you see?"

"Please tell us!"

"Caterpillars are always hungry," explains Sweetpea.
"They have to eat and eat and eat and eat!"
  "But my caterpillar said he only wanted one more leaf!"
says Rose.

"That means he'll turn into a chrysalis soon.
Then he won't need to eat at all," says Sweetpea.
    "What's a chrysalis?" asks Violet.
    "Wait and see!" Sweetpea replies.

When Rose gets back to her flower, there's another surprise for her. The caterpillar has gone, and hanging from the leaf on a silk thread is a shiny hard thing.

"Oh dear!" says Rose.

"What's happening now?" asks Violet.

Rose and Violet rush back to see Sweetpea.

"The caterpillar has spun a silk thread around himself.
He's turned into a chrysalis," she explains.

"Why?" asks Rose.

"Wait and see!" replies Sweetpea.

For fourteen days, Rose waits

and waits.

But she can't see anything!

And then, one morning, something magical happens.

Out of the shiny hard shell comes . . .

. . . a beautiful butterfly!

"Just think," Rose says proudly. "MY rose helped him to grow!"

The other Dewdrop Babies hurry to admire Rose's butterfly.

"Thank you, Rose!" says the butterfly, as it opens its wings and flies into the sunny garden.

"It's magical!"

For Ann and Chris,
Kate and Emma

SWEETPEA'S SURPRISE
A PICTURE CORGI BOOK 978 0 552 55653 8

First published in Great Britain by Picture Corgi,
an imprint of Random House Children's Books
A Random House Group Company

This edition published 2008

1 3 5 7 9 10 8 6 4 2

Text copyright © Random House Children's Books, 2008
Illustrations copyright © Patricia MacCarthy, 2008
Concept © Random House Children's Books and Patricia MacCarthy, 2008
Text by Alison Ritchie
Design by Tracey Cunnell

Picture Corgi Books are published by Random House Children's Books,
61-63 Uxbridge Road, London W5 5SA

www.dewdropbabies.com
www.rbooks.co.uk

Addresses for companies within The Random House Group Limited
can be found at: www.randomhouse.co.uk/offices.htm

THE RANDOM HOUSE GROUP Limited Reg. No. 954009

A CIP catalogue record for this book is available from the British Library.

Printed in China